Let's Go CANOEING and KAYAKING

Suzanne Slade

PowerKiDS press

New York

To my dad, who loves to canoe and kayak

Published in 2007 by The Rosen Publishing Group, Inc.
29 East 21st Street, New York, NY 10010

First Edition

Editor: Amelie von Zumbusch
Book Design: Dean Galiano and Erica Clendening
Layout Design: Julio Gil

Photo Credits: Cover © Raymond Gehman/Getty Images; pp. 4, 10, 15, 16, 17, 24, 25, 26 © www.shutterstock.com; p. 6 © www.istockphoto.com/ngirish; pp. 8, 12 © www.istockphoto.com/ Jeff Logan; p. 9 © www.istockphoto.com/Greg Nicholas; p. 13 © www.istockphoto.com/Paul Vasarhelyi; pp. 18, 19, 20, 29 © Getty Images; p. 21 Courtesy of Suzanne Slade; p. 22 © Wolfgang Kaehler/Corbis; p. 28 © www.istockphoto.com/Tim Furnas.

Library of Congress Cataloging-in-Publication Data

Slade, Suzanne.
  Let's go canoeing and kayaking / Suzanne Slade. — 1st ed.
      p. cm. — (Adventures outdoors)
  Includes index.
  ISBN-13: 978-1-4042-3649-3 (library binding)
  ISBN-10: 1-4042-3649-X (library binding)
  1. Canoes and canoeing—Juvenile literature. 2. Kayaking—Juvenile literature. I. Title.
  GV784.3.S53 2007
  797.1'22—dc22
                                2006019564

Manufactured in the United States of America

Contents

Canoeing and Kayaking

Canoeing is a great way to enjoy the beauty of nature while getting some exercise. You can paddle down a winding river or glide across a glassy lake. Canoeing is a sport you can do by yourself or with some friends. A person of any age or size can canoe. If you get tired while paddling, you can jump into the water and go for a swim.

In a canoe you can travel to interesting places. You can learn about animals in the water and discover new kinds of fish. On nearby land you might see raccoons, blue jays, deer, and woodpeckers. You can feed the ducks or geese that swim by. There is a lot to see and do when you go canoeing.

DID YOU KNOW?

One special kind of canoe is the kayak. Kayaks are canoes with covered tops that have small holes for people to sit in.

These people are using a canoe to explore New Zealand's Whanganui River.

Where to Go Boating

It's a good idea to make a plan before your canoe trip. Nearby lakes, rivers, and ponds are excellent places to go canoeing. Look for Private Property or No **Trespassing** signs so you can avoid private water that could be unsafe. Many public lakes and rivers have a **ramp** where you can **launch** a boat. Some launching areas charge a small fee to put your boat in the water.

If you want an exciting, adventurous canoe trip, a fast-moving river is a great choice for you. A quiet pond is the perfect place if you feel like relaxing. You can go to a lake if you want to get some exercise, go exploring, or visit with other boaters.

You can launch a canoe from this floating dock at Fundy National Park, in New Brunswick, Canada.

Boating Gear

The right gear will help you have a smooth and safe canoeing trip. The most important thing you will need is a life jacket. Every person in the boat should wear a properly fitting life jacket. You should also bring a hat and sunscreen. Paddling a boat can be tiring, so pack plenty of food and water for your trip.

Life jackets come in different shapes, sizes, and colors.

A canoe is a great way to get closer to the fish you are trying to catch.

If the day is cool, you should take an extra jacket and dry clothes in case you get wet. On hot days pack a swimsuit so you can cool off in the lake. A net and fishing pole will come in handy if you want to catch a fish or turtle. To capture the beautiful sights and memories, bring your camera along, too.

Learning to Canoe

Most canoes have two seats and can hold from one to four people. One person sits at the **stern** of the boat. A second person can sit in the canoe's **bow**. The people in the bow and stern do the paddling. Passengers sit on the floor in the middle of the canoe. Canoes tip over easily. When getting in or out of a canoe, move slowly and keep your weight in the center of the boat.

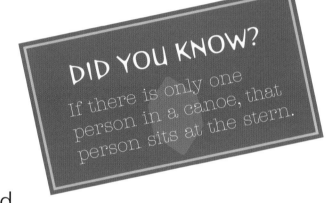

DID YOU KNOW?

If there is only one person in a canoe, that person sits at the stern.

Canoe paddles are made of wood, plastic, or other human-made **materials**. It's important to choose the right-size paddle. When standing beside your paddle, the handle should be somewhere

Some canoes, like this one, have seats with backs. Other canoes have flat seats.

The person in the stern and the person in the bow usually paddle on opposite sides of the canoe.

between your eyes and mouth. To hold your paddle, grab the shaft with one hand and grip the top with the other.

There are three basic paddling strokes. To move forward place the entire **blade** in the water at a right angle to the canoe. Pull back on the paddle while keeping it close beside the boat. To move sideways turn the paddle blade so it faces you. Place the paddle out in the water as far as you can and pull it toward you. The person in the stern can turn right by using the paddle to make a C-shaped stroke to the left. A C-stroke to the right will make the canoe turn left. If two people are paddling a canoe, the person at the stern does the steering. The person in the bow often sets the pace, or speed, of the paddling.

Although canoes can carry several people, you need only one person to paddle a canoe.

White-Water Canoeing

White-water canoeing is fun and challenging. Adventurous boaters get to canoe through fast-moving white water in this exciting sport.

You need special training, skills, and gear before you can go white-water canoeing. Along with a life jacket, you must also wear a **helmet**. When canoeing in white water, you often get wet. Wearing **goggles** will help you see. A rain jacket will keep you dry and warm.

You should also know how to read a river, or be able to spot signs of danger in the water ahead. You need to steer quickly around large rocks and fallen trees on a white-water course.

DID YOU KNOW?

Some people like to race on white-water courses. During these high-speed events, boaters steer their canoes around gates, or poles. On some courses the racers must paddle against the flow of the river in certain places.

These white-water canoeists are on the Ottawa River.

Canoeing and Camping

If you want to take a long canoe trip, take along some extra supplies and camp for a few nights. As you drift down a river, you can set up camp in a different place each night.

Pack a tent, food, sleeping bags, pillows, bug spray, matches, and dry clothing for camping. When you find your camping spot, tie up your canoe

A canoe is an easy way to move your camping gear from one campsite to another.

The campers who set up these tents reached their campsite with special canoes called kayaks.

securely with a rope or pull it up on the shore. Choose a flat, dry location to pitch your tent. Before setting up your tent, clear the area of rocks and sticks. If you want to start a campfire, find a safe place far from trees or dry plants. A meal cooked over a fire will taste great after a day of canoeing.

Early Canoes

People have been making canoes for thousands of years. The first canoes were used for travel. Early Native Americans made two types of canoes. They used trees to create solid, one-piece canoes called **dugout canoes**. They formed the sitting area by carving a large hole in the center of a log. Then they shaped and smoothed the canoe's outside.

The second type of Native American canoe has a frame made of strong pieces of wood. Native

This picture shows canoes at a Native American camp along California's Merced River.

This 1867 painting shows Native American women harvesting wild rice in their canoe.

Americans in the North stretched the skins of large animals, such as moose and **caribou**, over the wood frame. Canoes built in the East were often covered with bark from birch or elm trees. Native Americans living in the Arctic used walrus skins on their canoes.

19

Kayaking

Kayaks and open canoes have many similarities, but they also have several differences. A kayak has a covered top, called a deck. Kayaks have one or two holes, called cockpits, in the deck. The passenger sits in the cockpit. Some kayakers wear a cover called a spraydeck to keep dry. A spraydeck fits around the kayaker's waist and fastens to the kayak.

These people are kayaking at the lake in New York City's Central Park.

You need a special kayak built for two people if you want to kayak with a friend or relative.

A kayak paddle has a blade on each end. You hold the paddle with your hands slightly more than shoulder width apart. To begin paddling extend your arms and hold the paddle in front of you. Then dip one blade in the water near your feet. Pull the blade back, turn your body, and place the other blade in the water.

The First Kayaks

Thousand of years ago, the Yupik and Inuit peoples created the first kayaks. The Yupiks and Inuits are native peoples of the Arctic. They are often called Eskimos. They used kayaks to travel and to hunt for food.

Eskimos built kayaks from animal bones, **driftwood**, and sealskins. They built a sturdy frame from wood and bones. Then they stretched sealskin over it. They sewed the skins together using string made from seal **sinews**. To make the kayaks float better, they put air-filled animal **bladders** under the sealskin.

DID YOU KNOW?

If your kayak flips over, use your paddle to do an Eskimo roll. The Eskimos invented this move. It let them turn their kayaks upright quickly when they kayaked through icy waters.

This Inuit man is paddling a kayak near Southampton Island in Canada's Northwest Territories.

Sea Kayaking

People use sea kayaks on ocean waters. A sea kayak is not as deep as a regular kayak. It has a shallow body, which allows it to move in close to shore. This long, sleek boat travels quietly through the water. You can use a sea kayak to get near birds and animals in the ocean.

Some people like to take their sea kayaks on long trips. The front of a sea kayak has several hatches,

Sea kayaking is also known as ocean kayaking.

Some sea kayaks, like the one above, are built to carry two people.

where food, water, clothing, or a small tent can be stored. It's important to watch the weather when you go sea kayaking. Storms and high waves can cause big problems for this small craft.

Canoeing, Kayaking, and Nature

Canoeing and kayaking are great ways to explore nature. You can observe many types of animals while boating. Canoes and kayaks allow you to go into shallow areas where larger boats can't go. These small boats are powered by people instead of engines. This makes them quiet. You can approach animals without scaring them. Listen for the calls of different birds while you are drifting down a river. Watch for turtles poking their heads above the water for air or frogs resting on the shore. If you look closely, you might see fish swimming deep in the water.

Canoes and kayaks don't use fuel, so they don't pollute. Also, unlike boats with fast-moving blades, they won't hurt animals in the water.

Canoes and kayaks are great ways to get a close look at waterbirds, such as geese and ducks.

Let's Go Canoeing!

When you go canoeing, you can choose the trip that's right for you. Some people like to fish all day, while others like to stop for a long lunch.

Many people enjoy canoeing down a river. If something blocks your path on a river trip, such as a fallen tree or dam, you can portage. Portaging is

Unlike most other boats, canoes and kayaks are fairly light and easy to carry.

Canoeing is a great activity to do with a friend. These boys are canoeing in Fairfax County, Virginia.

when you carry your canoe across land. A canoe is light and easy to carry. You can place it back in the water to continue your trip. Wherever you choose to canoe, the smell of fresh air and the sound of water lapping against your boat will be relaxing.

Canoeing is a sport that everyone can enjoy, so let's go canoeing!

Safety Tips

- Always wear a life jacket that fits properly while canoeing and kayaking. Be sure to keep it fastened while you are on the water.

- Place your paddle across the sides of a canoe before you get in it. Lean on the paddle and keep your weight low as you slowly move into the boat.

- Never stand up in a canoe while you are out on the water.

- If you tip over in a canoe, remain calm and swim back to the canoe. Even though it is turned over, it will still float.

- Don't go down a river that looks unsafe or has water that is moving too fast.

- Always canoe or kayak with a buddy.

- Make sure you take plenty of water to drink when you go out on a boat. You need to drink often when you are paddling and out in the hot sun.

- Do not canoe or kayak near swimmers. Canoes and kayaks are large and heavy and you cannot stop them quickly.

- Obey signs that mark a closed trail or unsafe area.

- You should know how to turn a kayak upright if it flips over. Before going out in a kayak, practice your rolls. Make sure a knowledgeable adult is present when you are practicing.

Glossary

bladders (BLA-derz) The parts of bodies that store urine.

blade (BLAYD) The wide, flat part of an oar or paddle.

bow (BOW) The forward part of a ship or boat.

caribou (KER-eh-boo) Large deer that live in the North American Arctic.

driftwood (DRIFT-wuhd) Wood that washes up on the shore.

dugout canoes (DUG-owt kuh-NOOZ) Narrow boats made from hollowed-out logs that move through the water by paddling.

goggles (GOG-elz) A kind of eyeglasses that fit close around your eyes.

helmet (HEL-mit) A covering worn to keep the head safe.

launch (LONCH) To push out or to put into the air or water.

materials (muh-TEER-ee-ulz) What something is made of.

ramp (RAMP) A sloping platform.

sinews (SIN-yooz) Strong bands that join muscle to bone.

stern (STERN) The rear end of a ship or boat.

trespassing (TRES-pas-ing) Entering an area without permission.

Index

A
animals, 5, 19, 24, 27

B
blade, 12, 21
bow, 11, 13

C
caribou, 19

D
deck, 20
driftwood, 23
dugout canoes, 18

E
exercise, 5, 7

F
fish, 5, 9, 27
friends, 5

G
goggles, 14

H
helmet, 14

L
lake(s), 5, 7, 9

life jacket, 8, 14

M
materials, 11

N
nature, 5, 27

R
river(s), 7, 16, 28

S
signs, 7
sinews, 23
stern, 11, 13

Web Sites

Due to the changing nature of Internet links, PowerKids Press has developed an online list of Web sites related to this book. This site is updated regularly. Please use this link to access the list: www.powerkidslinks.com/adout/canoeing/